The Late Reindeer by Chris Allton

For Layla and Oliver

Chapter 1

Have you ever heard of Rudolph the red-nosed reindeer? Of course you have. He is the most famous reindeer of all. He has a very shiny nose and all of the other reindeer love him. And why wouldn't they? He saved Christmas by guiding Santa with his nose.

To start with, Rudolph was very shy and kept himself to himself. Why? All the other reindeers used to laugh at him. It was only because of bad weather one year and Santa needing help to lead the sleigh that you know all about him. There are seven other main reindeer but I bet you can't name them. Do you think you can? Ok, go for it. Rudolph...

1. Dasher
2. Prancer
3. Vixen
4. comet
5. cupid
6. Donner
7. Blitzen

How did you get on? I bet you have been singing that song to try and remember. Or maybe someone has helped you. Let's see how you did. We have mentioned Rudolph at number one but who else is there.

1. Dasher

Dasher is one of the fastest reindeer and he loves sewing. He is a whizz on a sewing machine and loves knitting. However, every time he makes a jumper for one of the other reindeers, it always ends in tears. Imagine trying to get a jumper over those antlers. He got his name from the German word "Dascher" which means 'purse maker'.

2. Prancer

This reindeer is so vain and loves himself so much. If he isn't strutting around the elves workshop king for attention, he can be found in front of a mirror flattening tufts of fur or polishing his antlers. Despite this he is a very loyal reindeer (probably because he is being a creep in front of Santa).

3. Vixen

Magic is Vixen's party trick. He loves to put on a magic show and entertain the other reindeers and elves. He once tried to put an elf in a box and cut him in half but the elf was so short, he didn't fill the box, so when he cut through, he missed the elf completely. He also likes to play tricks on the other reindeer (more about that later).

4. Comet

Comet is really laid back. So laid back he is almost lying down.   He loves playing football with the fawns and they all look up to him as he is full of words of wisdom and setting an example of good behaviour.

5. Cupid

Cupid is a very loving reindeer. She always has a piece of mistletoe hanging from her antlers. The good thing about Cupid is her baking skills, especially the mince pies she makes. Santa loves her mince pies and he can often be found hanging around the kitchen and stuffing the tasty treats into his pocket. The bad thing about Cupid? Her singing! It is terrible. If you want to empty a room, then just ask Cupid to sing some carols. Her voice has been known to shatter glass, once shattering Santa's glasses (he wasn't happy).

6. Donner

Every time Donner enters a room, he does so with a big, deep booming voice. In fact, you can hear him coming before he even enters a room. His name means 'thunder' and that is what it sounds like. Like Cupid, he loves singing but luckily, he is a great singer especially when he does duets with his twin, Blitzen.

7. Blitzen

Donner's twin, Blitzen is always on time. His name means 'lightning' and it matches his speed as along with Dasher, he is one of the fastest reindeer around. When he gets together with his brother, they love to sing songs by Elvis Presley.

So those are Santa's main reindeer. His first eight. The first names on the team list. There are of course many other reindeer: it's a big job getting Santa ready for Christmas Eve, but they are the famous ones who everyone knows. Like celebrities on "Strictly" or "I'm a celebrity".

Our story involves these reindeer but there is one more we need to mention. This reindeer is called Layla and she is always late.

Chapter 2

It's not her fault. Or that's what she says anyway. But if we look at the evidence, you will have to agree she is always late. Let's look at her typical day.

In the morning, the alarm goes off in the stable and what does Layla do? She presses the snooze button…. Several times! She then takes forever to brush her fur and because of this she never gets round to polishing her antlers so they always look a bit dirty and like mould is growing on them.

By the time Layla gets to breakfast most of the other reindeer have finished their food. Vixen likes to hide her bowl so she spends five minutes looking for it, making her even later. She then has her porridge (eventually) but she doesn't like it too hot, so she waits for it to cool down, taking even more time.

At this point in the day (about nine o'clock) Layla is already fifteen minutes behind. This doesn't please Oliver who is the reindeer she works with. Layla is young in comparison to Oliver. He is an older, wise reindeer.

Oliver has been with Santa a long, long, LONG time. Probably longer than any reindeer Layla thought. She thought he was a bit grumpy but she put this down to him being old.

A lot of Oliver's fur was turning grey now and he had a little bald patch between his antlers. He and Layla work in the reindeer dust department and he puts up with Layla's lateness every day. Layla thinks he is too old to be working there as she thinks he keeps forgetting things or asking her to do pointless jobs.

However, Oliver is very experienced and knows exactly what he is doing as he only wants the best for Layla. She is just a bit young to realise it yet.

Layla is a little different to all the other reindeers. She looks different and she acts different. To start off with she has a different nose to everyone else. Now Rudolph has a red nose (and a song named after him) but Layla has a white nose – as white as the snow underground – a no song named after her.

This makes her stand out amongst all the reindeer and this is something she doesn't like.

Initially it was nice to have a different coloured nose but she soon realised how Rudolph felt as he was picked on (until he saved Christmas one year) then everyone thought he was the best. Following that, they thought they would pick on Layla and her nose as she stood out.

They call her snowy nose or white tip. They say her nose was a different colour because she picks it so much but she doesn't (at least not while anyone is looking). They mock her saying she isn't as good as Rudolph as she doesn't have a song.

The other feature of Layla that stands out is her left ear. It is completely white unlike the rest of her which is light brown (normal reindeer colour). She often wondered why her ear was like this but nothing came to mind. She asked Oliver about it but he just said it was because she was special.

"Special?" Layla replied, "I don't want to be special."

"Well you are Layla, and you always will be," Oliver explained.

Along with always being late, Layla kept herself to herself most of the time. She was a bit of a loner and preferred her own company to others. When she finished work with Oliver, she would often take walks out on the ice plains or hide away in her stable from al the other reindeer. Even though she thought Oliver was a bit old and made her do unpleasant things, he was her only real friend, but that pleased her no end. Some of the other reindeer were a little annoying and Layla thought it would be better to just keep out of their way.

Anyway, back to her usual day. Layla is running late after breakfast. She puts her plate and spoon back in the kitchen and wanders back to the stable, taking as much time as possible.

"The longer I take, the less time I'll have to spend at work," she thought to herself, thinking she was a clever little reindeer.

On this particular day, she passed the football field and could see Comet playing football with a huge pack of fawns. They just swarmed around the ball charging after it all over the pitch. Layla laughed to herself as she could see disaster about to strike. It always did – nearly every day.

Sure enough, there was a loud pop. The ball had lifted into the air and landed on a poor fawn's antlers. Game over. As Comet tried to console the crying fawn, Layla continued chuckling to herself and headed towards work.

Chapter 3

"You're late...again!" Oliver complained as she entered the reindeer dust department.

"If I'm always late, you should be used to it by now," Layla replied sarcastically. She laughed to herself as she put on her apron. She loved her apron as it made her smile. On the front of it was the body of an elf so when she put it on, it looked like an elf with a reindeer head.

The reindeer dust department was a large area. There were vast storage containers one after the other, containing every colour of reindeer dust imaginable. Each one the size of two houses but with a tiny tap on the front of each to test the reindeer dust. This was Oliver's job and Layla was his apprentice (this means she copied and learnt what Oliver did). Although the containers were vast, the two reindeer were the only ones around most of the day.

"We have to check container 45. The console says there is a potential blockage that needs sorting," Oliver announced.

"Great, isn't that one miles away?" moaned Layla. Oliver shook his head.

"You are a lazy late reindeer aren't you. It will take twenty minutes to walk there. The exercise will do us good," came the response. Oliver picked up his satchel and they set off down long repetitive corridors past vat after vat of reindeer dust. Layla counted in her head as they passed each one. After ten minutes, they passed container 22.

"Halfway there," offered Oliver enthusiastically, but the look on Layla's face said everything.

"Halfway? Great," she moaned.

Eventually they arrived at the container, on its

side in huge letters read

"So what's wrong with it?" Layla questioned.

"It looks ok to me."

"Well, you obviously haven't been listening to

all the things I have taught you, have you? The

console back in the office has been lit up like a

Christmas tree all morning. There must be a blockage inside so you know what that means."

As he said this a grin appeared over Oliver's face. This was not copied by Layla as she knew exactly what was coming next.

"No, I'm not doing it!" barked Layla.

"You are," came the reply. Layla sighed and huffed but no change. She hated this part of the job. So did Oliver but now he had an apprentice he didn't have to worry about what was about to happen, it was Layla's problem now. "Up you go."

Layla pulled a face as if to say, "Why is it always me?" and trudged over to the side of the container. Each one was made of glass and was packed full of reindeer dust. This one had snow-white reindeer dust in and there was a blockage somewhere inside. Layla came to a ladder on the side of the container and reluctantly started the climb, very slowly.

"Are you sure you don't want to take a go?" she called down to Oliver.

"No, I'm fine here thank you very much. You just enjoy it," Oliver replied with a grin on his face.

Layla reached the top of the container and carefully walked across the top until she reached a hatch in the middle. There was a large wheel which she needed to turn. She knelt down and began turning the iron wheel. It creaked and squeaked loudly as it rotated. Layla was always apprehensive at this time as she knew what would happen and sure enough... as the wheel turned air passed into the container and a plume of reindeer dust shot into the air past Layla's face. She felt a thin layer of rainbow dust across her fur.

This was nothing though in comparison to what would come next. Layla had to lower herself into the container. This meant she would be covered in white reindeer dust for day – another reason why all the other reindeers made fun of her.

She carefully sat on the lip of the entrance and began to lower herself in, but as she did, she lost her footing and slipped into the gap – headfirst. "Great, just what I need," thought Layla.

The blockage was likely to be in the main pipe at the back of the container so Layla had to swim/climb through the reindeer dust to find it.

Finally reaching the pipe, she noticed a large blockage further down the pipe. She tried to reach the obstruction but with no luck.

After many attempts over five minutes, Layla eventually gave up and returned to the hatch. By now, Oliver had climbed up also and offered her a hand to pull her out.

"What's the problem?" he quizzed.

"There's something in the pipe but I can't move it," Layla responded.

"You better get out and get yourself cleaned up, you're a mess." Layla looked down at her paws and sure enough, they were completely white. If her paws were like that, the rest of her would be. Oh no!!

Chapter 4

Reindeer dust

For humans, reindeer dust is made from glitter and oats. They get their children to sprinkle this mixture either homemade or bought off the internet on the floor outside their house (never inside as glitter gets everywhere). However, this is not real reindeer dust.

Reindeer dust is only found at the North Pole. Have you heard of the Northern Lights? Maybe their other name – Aurora Borealis? These magical lights dance across the night sky in the Arctic with an array of colours. As they fly around the atmosphere, they gently touch mountains, icebergs and sometimes treetops. This is where the magic happens, this is where Reindeer dust is created.

Reindeer normally can't fly. There are only a select few who can. Obviously, Santa's first team of reindeer are included in this, along with any retired sleigh pullers. To be able to fly the chosen reindeer need to spend weeks of training in the northern lights to practise. When they reach the set standard, Santa picks the final selection and they then get their "wings", special harnesses that spread the dust.

Chosen reindeer use these harnesses to provide a steady supply of dust around them. This is what Oliver, and now Layla, have to collect. Oliver used to be able to fly, but now old age has caught up with him. Layla, even if she wanted to, couldn't fly. She was far too small to fit a special harness.

So, Layla's job was to collect this reindeer dust from the mountains, icebergs and treetops. To do this she had her own snowmobile with what looked like a giant hoover on the back. It was obviously a lot more technical than a hoover but you get the idea.

The SCOOP XR7i was a top of the range machine. Only the best for the North Pole and Santa. Only Oliver (being one of the oldest and wisest reindeer) was allowed to drive this. Layla always asked but she always got the same reply.

"No, you are far too small. When you are a little older, you will be able to learn to drive it," Oliver repeated over and over. This was not what Layla wanted to hear but it was what she had to put up with.

So, on evenings the Northern Lights appeared, the two of them set off in the SCOOP XR7i to collect reindeer dust. Oliver would be in the driving seat and Layla sat on a little box next to him (there was only one seat in this amazing machine, typical).

This particular evening, the night before Christmas Eve, Layla had cleaned herself after falling in the white container. She had got rid of most of the dust but bits were still up her nose and this caused her to sneeze regularly. This caused much hilarity for Oliver but as he pointed out he knew how she felt as it had happened to him when he was younger.

They were now travelling across the ice plain towards the Great North Iceberg, one of the largest in the world. Despite the Northern Lights being so large in the sky, the amount of reindeer dust produced is not as much. The collection of the SCOOP XR7i was therefore vital. The evening passed without incident and the pair returned to headquarters with a full tank.

When they approached the containers, Oliver reversed the SCOOP XR7i to the sorting plant. This really was the magical part. Amazing technology created by the elves. Oliver just connect the end of the large hoover to a machine and switched the machine to blow instead of suck. It all then just flies into the sorting plant and then by some scientific process involving different densities and weight of dust particles, they sort automatically to the correct containers.

The next step of the process is to filter it into finer dust ready to put on board the sleigh so it can be moved into the special reindeer harnesses when necessary.

So the dust began blowing into the correct sections. Oliver left Layla to complete this part of the process. He was tired – tired as he was one of the oldest reindeer and tired because Layla had persistently been asking to drive the SCOOP XR7i.

"Get on with the job in hand," he ordered. "It's Christmas Eve tomorrow." Layla begrudgingly did as she was told.

"I'll show him," she muttered under her breath as she continued with the task at hand.

Chapter 5

After about an hour, the SCOOP XR7i had finished blowing dust into the containers. Layla checked the machinery and was happy that everything was sorted, so set off back to the stables.

It was still dark: it was the early hours of the morning. Today was Christmas Eve. The most important day of the year in the North Pole. All the preparations for Santa's trip were in place. It had been planned for 365 days, since last

Christmas day. The elves had sorted all the presents and the sleigh was prepared. Santa's first team of reindeer were primed and ready for action. The reindeer dust would be ready to be dispersed through the special harnesses and Santa would soon be on his way. All the hard work Layla had put in all year (along with Oliver of course) was now done. Christmas Eve night was her night off.

As she passed the football field again, there were no fawns running around playing football like earlier. No everything seemed quiet. A fresh falling of snow meant that the floor looked like a white carpet, brand new and never stood upon.

As she rounded the far corner of the field, two familiar figures appeared in front of her – Rodney and Ralph.

Rodney and Ralph were twins – identical. They were a little older than Layla – teenage reindeer! They did not do much and tried to avoid any work whenever possible. They liked to act big in front of the smaller reindeer and picked on them whenever they could. Layla was in no mood for this at all so tried to walk in a different direction but they were having none of it.

"Here she is… Layla the lazy, late reindeer," laughed Rodney.

"Are you running late now?" sneered Ralph.

"Leave me alone, it's been a long night and today is my day off," came Layla's reply.

"Off to bed then, lazy Layla," mocked Rodney.

"I'm not lazy," growled Layla, getting a little annoyed with the bullies now.

"We have spoke to Oliver. He says you are in trouble for asking to drive the SCOOP XR7i," Ralph suggested.

"No I am not!" argued Layla. She was getting more and more frustrated by her tormentors and had had enough.

"You are going to be replaced. We are taking your job from now on," Rodney explained.

"That's a lie," cried Layla, more and more agitated. She may have fallen out with Oliver, she may moan about her job, but it was her job and as far as she was concerned, no one was going to take it from her.

"It's not a lie, we have proof." With that Ralph pulled out a rolled-up scroll from a satchel around his neck. He read the following -

To whom it may concern...

As of today, Rodney and Ralph will be the new assistants for collecting reindeer dust.

Merry Christmas

Santa

Layla could not believe this. No wonder Oliver would not let her drive the SCOOP XR7i. To lose her job was bad enough but to have these two take over from her. That was too much.

Tears started to run down Layla's face: she couldn't hold it back.

"Oh look, the lazy, late and now jobless reindeer is crying. What a big baby." Rodney and Ralph laughed out loud.

Layla started to get angry – she couldn't take anymore. Disappointment was being overtaken by anger. She lowered her head and made her antlers point towards the bullies.

"Ha ha ha, look at her now," the bullies called out but Layla wasn't laughing she charged as fast as she could at the two, naughty reindeer. Their laughter soon turned to panicked cried. No matter the size of reindeer, a set of antlers rammed into you is not nice. They turned and ran off.

Layla stopped. Her anger had subsided and now the tears returned. She could not believe what had happened to her. She asked herself over and over what had gone on to make this happen. Had she said something to Oliver to upset him? Had she upset Santa? Maybe she shouldn't have asked to drive the SCOOP XR7i. Whatever it was she was struggling to cope with it.

"If they don't want me doing the job I do, then I will leave. I don't know where I'll go but if I'm not wanted here, I'll be better off anywhere but here," Layla thought to herself.

She carefully sneaked back to the stables and packed a satchel: a selection of carrots, a picture of Oliver and her reindeer bell that Santa had given her. All reindeer had a small bell and the further they progressed the bigger the bell they got. It was, along with the picture of Oliver, her most prized possession.

The sun was beginning to rise over the large iceberg to the east so Layla needed to be away before everyone else rose from their night's sleep.

Chapter 6

Once she had been walking for about an hour, Layla was confident she would be a safe distance to stop and have a snack. She was at the edge of Frozen Forest and found a tree trunk that had fallen to the floor. She jumped up, perched on the edge of it and opened her satchel and chose a small carrot.

"I need to keep these going for a few days," she mumbled to herself. Once she had finished the measly morsel, she continued her walk along the edge of the forest. The plan of leaving seemed the only answer a few hours ago, but now the reality of being on her own, in a frozen wilderness, was hitting home quickly and she ked the idea less and less.

As she walked, she thought carefully about what she had left behind. She missed Oliver, but was cross that he had replaced her. She missed her job, even though she moaned about it none stop. And she missed Santa... Santa!!! Oh no. Today was the most important day in the year and she had left. Everyone came together on Christmas Eve to wave goodbye to Santa before he set off on his sleigh, but here she was, miles away from home and definitely no Santa around.

She began to cry. Layla didn't realise quite how much until she became aware of another presence around her. Twigs were cracking in the Frozen Forest and suddenly her tears seemed much further away and unwanted. Now fear and apprehension was what she felt as she started to move a little faster.

Up ahead she could see some rocks. These giant boulders looked like teeth popping out of the white mouth below. Not only would they provide shelter a perhaps a place to stay for the night, but also providing high ground so she could keep an eye out for unwanted visitors.

Snow wolves roamed the edge of the forest, looking for a quick snack, darting out from the cover of the forest, catching their prey and dragging them back into the forest. Layla did not like the idea of this and, despite wolves not usually attacking packs of reindeer, she didn't feel quite as confident on the own.

The rocks became closer and closer as Layla sped up, the feeling someone watching her grew more and more. Finally, the rocks were in front of her and she headed into a dark cave to get some shelter. As she entered, she heard heavy breathing and grunts and groans.

"Yikes, who's in here?" Layla pondered. Her question was soon answered as a giant shadow grew in front of her. There, growing in stature was the form of a polar bear. Layla backed out of the cave and back into the white abyss behind her. "I'll take my chances in the forest," she thought.

This decision was not much better for as she turned around, the owner of the grunts and broken twigs was before her. There stood a huge snow wolf, snarling and licking its lips. Layla turned again and there was the polar bear, now reared up on its hind legs, heading for her. Could this day get any worse?

Layla didn't know what to do and her natural reaction was to curl up and close her eyes. She had accepted she would be someone's dinner.

Loud roars and growls followed. There was the sound of a scuffle and after what seemed ages, the sound of whimpering disappearing into the distance. Layla opened her eyes. There stood the polar bear – victorious. Layla felt sure she would be next in the fight but instead the giant bear just stood and looked at her. What was he thinking? Layla thought. As he returned to all fours and turned Layla instantly knew what it was. There, behind the Daddy bear was a tiny baby polar bear - a cub.

"Hello, are you ok?" the cub asked.

"I am yes, thank you," Layla responded.

"My name is Percy," the polar bear continued, "and that was my dad. We heard you coming into our cave and thought you were the wolf. He's been waiting for me to come out of the cave my dad says. But I say in for now to keep safe.

What are you doing out here on your own? Where is the rest of your herd?"

"I'm all alone," Layla replied, holding back the tears.

"Poor thing. I thought you might be, that's why I sent Dad out to help you."

"Thank you so so much."

"Not a problem, I'm sure you would have done the same for me. Now why are you out here all alone?" Layla explained the story of what had happened and how she missed home and wanted to get back to see Santa but felt like no one wanted her.

"I bet they are all worried about you back home. Once I wandered off and left my Dad because we had had an argument but I missed him so much. He was going out of his mind with worry," Percy continued. "Just go back."

By now the light was starting to fade. As it was winter, there weren't many hours of daylight at this time of year. Layla had not thought of this and along with everything else, she slumped on the floor and cried.

"Don't worry," comforted Percy, "we can still make this all ok. My dad will give you a lift home on his back. He is very comfy and if he knows you work for Santa, he'll be delighted to help."

"Thank you so much," Layla replied. "I'm ready to go home now."

Chapter 7

Percy's dad didn't mess around. He was the perfect taxi home and took the quickest route. Direct. This involved climbing over hills, rocks and mountains. As Layla and Percy hung on to the giant furry transport, she could see the Northern lights, glowing up the night sky.

"That's what I collect," Layla announced to Percy and his dad.

"We know," replied Percy. Layla was confused. How could they possibly know what Layla did, they hadn't asked before now.

"How?" Layla questioned.

"It's obvious, look at your antlers," came the reply. Layla couldn't. As they were on the top of her head, she could see nothing.

"I can't see," she responded. Percy laughed to himself.

"They're glowing in the dark. You are like a torch on four legs." Layla couldn't believe this. It must have been the reindeer dust and a lack of cleaning her antlers. Because of this, they must glow in the dark. She must be covered in the dust. All this time and she never knew.

"Look, dad is using you as a light." Layla could see this now and smiled to herself. Perhaps she was some use to others after all. The journey back was treacherous as the weather had got much, much worse. They trudged on through the darkness and Layla soon realised she would not be back in time to see Santa before he left.

"We are nearly there," Percy's Dad shouted through the wind and the snow. "Look, there's something ahead. I can see a light."

Sure enough, they could see a light faintly through the blizzard. As they got closer, Layla could see the familiar shape and antlers of Oliver. She jumped off the bear's back and ran through the snow. He opened up his front paws and the pair hugged as if they hadn't seen each other for a year.

"Where have you been? I have been so worried." He gasped thankfully.

"I didn't think you wanted me around anymore. You, Santa, everyone."

"You silly little reindeer," he smiled at her. "I couldn't do my job without you. I'm old and you are ready to take over. That's why I told Santa to promote you. You're the head of Reindeer Dust now, in charge of those two fools Rodney and Ralph."

"I thought they were replacing me," sighed Layla. Suddenly, everything fit into place. "Oh... I am a silly reindeer aren't I."

"That you are Layla, that you are," Oliver replied.

Suddenly, a loud siren went off. Both Layla and Oliver knew what this meant. It was the Christmas Eve emergency siren. It meant something was wrong with Santa's plans for the night.

"We need to get back. There is a problem and it could be something only we can fix," Oliver ordered. "It's going to take us ages in this snow."

"Not if I have anything to do with it. Percy's dad announced. "Jump on, I'll get you there in no time." The pair of reindeer climbed onto the back of the gigantic beast and before they knew it, they were moving through the thick snow, like a giant snowplough, back to headquarters.

Chapter 8

Elves are very good at technical things. Experts in fact. Their organisation system to make toys and organise presents is second to none. If you ever get the chance to visit the North Pole you would not believe how they get things done. Such effective workers. However, put a polar bear in front of them and it's a different story.

As the polar bear strode into the square in front of Santa Headquarters, elves scattered in every direction. An elf is between one and two-foot tall whereas a polar could be ten feet tall. They feared they would be trampled on so ran for their lives.

Oliver led Layla into the main building and they entered the huge communications room – Mission Control. Red flashing lights blinked everywhere and the siren was still deafening anyone with a mile of the facility.

"Turn that siren off!" ordered Oliver. "That's the last thing we need at this moment." Elves rushed around and within seconds, the sirens ended. The sound of murmuring elves filled the air.

"Right, what is the problem," quizzed Oliver.

Eric, one of the head elves, appeared with a clipboard in front of him and a headset into which he was talking frantically.

"Sir, there is a present missing."

"What? How is this possible?" Oliver demanded. "You have been planning this all year."

"We are still trying to figure this out," replied the elf.

"Well get on with it then, find out where it has gone. Layla, you go back to our station and check everything is ok there. We don't want any other mistakes."

Layla followed his instructions and thought now would not be the time to question him. As she entered the reindeer dust department, she noticed flashing lights on the console. The blockage! She wondered if this was anything to do with the problems at mission control. Maybe a blocked pipe was a small part of a large machine.

Layla decided to investigate. She went back to the white container and climbed the ladder slowly. She was very tired from her excursion outside but the adrenalin was pumping through her body and she was determined to get the job done. Again she turned the wheel and lifted the hatch. There seemed even more dust in now but Layla knew what she had to do.

She carefully lowered herself in and waded through the container. The dust was everywhere and she could hardly see her paws in front of her. She made her way to the pipe and reached her paw in. Again, the blockage was still there. What on earth was it? Perhaps part of the machine or the SCOOP XR7i. She hoped not. Oliver would go mad at that.

She couldn't grab it but it was obvious this was a problem. There was only one thing to do. Layla would have to climb into the pipe and try pushing it back the way it had come in. This could be dangerous as she could get stuck permanently but it was a risk she was willing to take.

Being a smaller reindeer, Layla's antlers were not fully formed or grown yet. Very few other reindeer would be able to fit in so she was perfect.

The tube was tight, very tight, but the antlers were flexible and moved well. She reached the blockage and was able to feel it a bit more. She felt something round, then some spokes. It was a wheel. As she moved further up, she felt a seat and a pedal. It was a bike! What on earth was a bike doing in the entrance pipe of the white, reindeer dust container. At the moment, why did not matter, she needed to love it. As she pushed with her paw, she could not move the obstruction. Then she had an idea.

She got on all fours in the pipe as best she could and attacked the bike with her antlers. This gave her grip with her paws and the ability to push with her head. It was working. As she pushed and pushed the bike inched its way out. Little by little Layla was able to move the bike with her antlers. Sometimes pushing the back wheel, sometimes the seat. The further she went, Layla soon realised she would end up at the entrance to the machine where the SCOOP XR7i would blow the dust in.

Sure enough out the bike came first followed by Layla. She was now whiter than she had ever been before. Covered antler to toe in white reindeer dust. She went to the console and picked up the phone to contact Mission Control.

"Who's that?" questioned Layla.

"It's Eric," came the reply.

"I need to speak to Oliver," Layla demanded. "It's urgent."

"Unfortunately, he is dealing with a pair of naughty reindeer at the moment. Rodney and Ralph have broken into Santa's workshop at night and stolen a bike. They have tried to power it with reindeer dust so they can fly around on it."

"That explains why there is a bike stuck in my pipe. Tell Oliver I have got it out," Layla requested.

"I will, but there is another problem."

"What? Layla asked.

"We have had a message from Santa. He is struggling to keep altitude. There is a problem with the reindeer!"

Chapter 9

Layla wheeled the bike to Mission Control. Inside she could see Oliver reprimanding Rodney and Ralph very sternly. The two bullies couldn't look any different than earlier. Both had tears rolling down their face and shame and embarrassment to match.

"I have found your missing bike," Layla offered.

"Thanks," replied Oliver. "We have a bigger problem now too. Not only is Santa missing a present because of these two but we also have reindeer struggling to fly. Was there a problem with the reindeer dust?"

"Not that I know of," Layla answered.

"Right, we need to get this bike to Santa and an expert on reindeer dust. Any ideas?" Oliver asked. Layla smiled. She knew exactly what he meant.

"How on earth am I meant to get to Santa? I don't even know where he is."

"Well we can track Santa. At the moment he is travelling across Europe but he is way behind schedule as the reindeer can't fly as high as usual so they are having to fly more cautiously so they aren't seen," Oliver answered.

"And how exactly do I get there?" Layla quizzed. Oliver smiled.

"You still haven't got it yet have you. All these years at the dust department. How many hours have you spent in those containers? What happened to your antlers out on the ice plain when the Northern Lights appeared?" Layla was still confused.

"Well they glowed in the dark..." Oliver pressed her a little further.

"And why is that? You saw my antlers light up and yours do too. Who else's antlers do you know who light up? No one. We are special. You are special. Because of our exposure to reindeer dust our antlers glow."

"Wow," replied Layla astonished at her new skill.

"But that's not all Layla," Oliver replied. "You can fly."

Layla's mouth dropped. She couldn't believe this.

"Fly? But I don't have one of the special harnesses."

"You don't need one. You have been exposed to so much reindeer dust you don't need it. Watch." With this Oliver took two steps back away from Layla, the console and the other elves and reindeer around, who like Layla were equally gobsmacked by these new findings. Oliver closed his eyes and said a few lines like a spell.

"Reindeer dust, reindeer dust,

Even though we don't know why

Reindeer dust, reindeer dust,

Take me into the sky."

As he finished the words, the gathering crowd stood in awe as Oliver floated up into the air and circled Mission Control.

"Try it yourself," Oliver called down to Layla.

"But I can't do that," Layla answered.

"It's all about belief," he hollered back down, "you have to believe in yourself. Like I do. If you do that then you will be capable of anything. Don't forget the words."

With this Layla repeated the words –

"Reindeer dust, reindeer dust,

Even though we don't know why

Reindeer dust, reindeer dust,

Take me into the sky."

The next thing she knew, she was up in the air next to Oliver, screaming with excitement.

"This is amazing, I can't believe this," Layla yelled as she performed loops and spins through the air.

"You haven't got time for this. Eric, headset." With this Eric threw a headset into the air and Oliver caught it and placed it on Layla. "I can keep in contact with you using this. Grab that bike and get on your way."

With that, Layla ran through the air to the bike and sat upon it. She put her paws on the pedals and started pedalling and with a whoosh, she shot through the air, out of mission control and into the night sky.

Chapter 10

At first Layla thought she would be cold flying through the night sky but her fur and the dust kept her perfectly warm. The snowfall made it difficult to see but Oliver had set up a compass on the front of the bike that she could follow.

She climbed higher and higher above the clouds until she was in the still darkness of the night. Here, it was peaceful and still and she made good headway on her passage to Europe.

Instructions were regularly passed to her via the headset she wore and in no time, she could see lights of cities below her.

"You are almost there," Oliver announced. "Now Santa has told me he is currently awaiting your rescue on top of a hill called Rivington Pike. There is no one around as it is nearly midnight and no one goes hiking around midnight. Once you land, you will have to assess the situation and fix the problem. Is that clear?" Layla gulped.

"Yeah, no problem, I'll just save Christmas," she sarcastically replied. The compass on the front of the bike suddenly started flashing with the needle dancing around like it was at a disco. Layla could now see in the darkness, high above the lights of a small town, the lights of the sleigh and the faint glow of Rudolph's nose. She circled the top of the hill on the bike and carefully came into land.

She squeezed the breaks with a squeak and pulled up in front of Santa.

"I better put some oil on those brakes," Santa joked. "Thank you Layla, you have truly saved the day."

"Let's see if I can fix the reindeer dust first shall we," she replied, not wishing to be too optimistic at the start. "That bike needs cleaning and wrapping. I assume you have spare paper and tape in the sleigh? Of course you do, you're Santa." Santa gave a smile and ordered the twins, Donner and Blitzen to wrap the present and put the final product on the sleigh with the other presents.

This caused an argument between the two as to who would do what.

"You do the paper and I'll do the tape," ordered Donner in a booming voice.

"No, you do the paper and I'll do the tape," argued Blitzen.

"No."

"Yes."

"No!"

"Yes!"

"Oh for goodness sake, just wrap the present!" Layla interrupted, sick of the pointless bickering.

"Why should we listen to you, squirt?" Donner replied.

"Yeah Shorty, butt out of this. Why should we listen to you?" added Blitzen. Layla had now lost her patience.

"Because, you pair of pea-brains, I have just cycled here from the North Pole. I am now going to make it possible for you to fly, deliver all these presents and save Christmas." The pair soon changed their tune, not only through what she was saying but because as she spoke her antlers started glowing. Santa stood in the background, very quiet but with a huge smile on his face. He was so proud of the little reindeer, standing up for herself and for what she believed. It truly was inspirational to watch.

"How do you do that?" the reindeer questioned her. "I can't make my antlers glow."

"Well, how about this?" Layla replied as she started floating in the air. The reindeer couldn't believe what they were seeing.

"She's not wearing a harness. How is she doing this?" They all turned and whispered to each other unsure of what was going on. Rudolph came to the front to speak to her.

"I know how you make your antlers glow but I don't know how you are flying, but if you teach us, you can lead the sleigh for the rest of the night."

"Me?" Layla gasped. This was a great honour.

"Layla, we are in your hands. We will listen to you. Only you can save tonight," Rudolph continued.

Layla took her place at the front of the pack of reindeer.

"Right guys, you do not need the reindeer dust now, you just need a bit of belief. I believe in you, Santa believes in you, now just believe in yourself. Now pull."

The pack moved forward across the hilltop, Layla was taking off the ground and Rudolph's nose was glowing just behind her.

"Come on guys, believe. It's Christmas." Rudolph shouted. The edge of the hilltop was fast approaching and as they ran off the edge, Layla shouted in an inspirational voice...

"BELIEVE."

The sleigh shot up into the night sky. They had done it. The reindeer believed in themselves and Layla. As they flew off into the night sky, faster than ever with an extra reindeer, the sound of Santa filled the air...

"Ho, ho, ho."

The previous night had been, in the end, a tremendous success. Numerous records had been shattered including the fastest delivery of all time. Santa had personally thanks Layla for her hard work and attitude with a special medal.

Layla spoke to Oliver, who was so proud of his little apprentice, and he had some news for her.

"After your escapades last night, you are now head of reindeer dust. I shall enjoy my retirement knowing you are in charge. Just don't be late!"

More title by Chris Allton

About Chris

Chris started writing 'Steam' (his first attempt at writing) in March 2017 and completed it in the following November. 'Embarrassing Dad' began almost immediately after and was released early 2018. In August 2019, he released his third book, 'Terrible Teacher'. Not based on true events, of course! During lockdown, he has been busy working on mindful and well-being texts for all ages. He has published a book for children entitled "Be Kind Kids" offering positive advice he has used in his teacher career or as a parent. A series of well-being journals have been published for kids, teachers and, well, anyone (everyone needs a bit of well-being don't they).

Printed in Great Britain
by Amazon